The Town Mouse and the Country Mouse

and Other Fables

Compiled by Vic Parker

 Gareth Stevens
PUBLISHING

Please visit our website, **www.garethstevens.com**. For a free color catalog of all our high-quality books, call toll free 1-800-542-2595 or fax 1-877-542-2596

Parker, Vic.
The town mouse and the country mouse and other fables / compiled by Vic Parker.
p. cm. — (Aesop's fables)
Includes index.
ISBN 978-1-4824-1320-5 (pbk.)
ISBN 978-1-4824-1260-4 (6-pack)
ISBN 978-1-4824-1461-5 (library binding)
1. Fables — Juvenile literature. 2. Aesop's fables — Adaptations — Juvenile literature.
I. Aesop. II. Parker, Victoria. III. Title.
PZ8.2 P37 2015
398.2—d23

Published in 2015 by
Gareth Stevens Publishing
111 East 14th Street, Suite 349
New York, NY 10003

Publishing Director Belinda Gallagher
Creative Director Jo Cowan
Editorial Director Rosie McGuire
Designer Joe Jones

ACKNOWLEDGEMENTS
The publishers would like to thank the following artists who have contributed to this book:
Cover: Natalie Hinrichsen at Advocate Art; Advocate Art: Natalie Hinrichsen, Tamsin Hinrichsen;
The Bright Agency: Marcin Piwowarski; Frank Endersby; Marco Furlotti; Jan Lewis (decorative frames)

Printed in the United States of America

CPSIA compliance information: Batch CS15GS: For further information contact Gareth Stevens, New York, New York at 1-800-542-2595.

Contents

The Crab
and the Fox

There was once a crab who lived in a rock pool at the seashore. But he grew bored and restless, seeing the same surroundings all the time. He wanted a change of scenery, so he left the beach and went inland, scurrying sideways.

There, he found a meadow, which he thought looked beautiful – lush and green, and filled with flowers. He settled

4

there, hoping it would be a good place to live.

But soon a hungry fox came along, and caught the crab. The fox had never seen a crab before and thought he smelled delicious! Just as he was going to be eaten up, the crab said, "This is what I deserve, for I had no business to leave my natural home by the sea and settle here as though I belonged to the land."

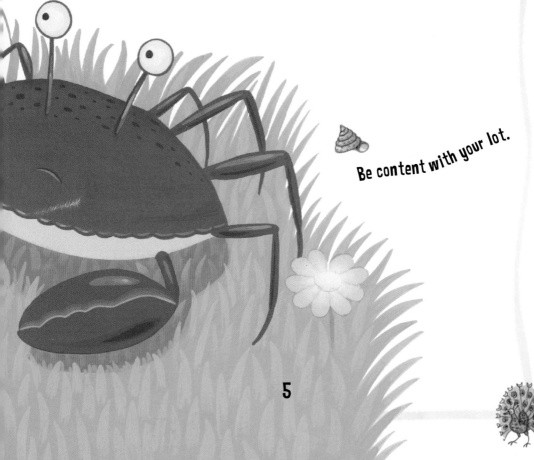

Be content with your lot.

5

The **Crow** and the **Pitcher**

There was once a crow who had been unable to find water for many days – not even a drop. He was half-dead with thirst, and barely had the energy to hop along the ground. Imagine his amazement and joy when he suddenly came upon a water pitcher.

However, when the crow put its beak into the mouth of the pitcher he found that very little water was left and that he could not reach far enough down to get at it. He tried and tried, but at last had to give up in despair.

The crow knew that he had no energy to go further in search of water, and death must surely be near. A sudden thought occurred to him, and he took a pebble and dropped it into the pitcher. Then he took another pebble and dropped it in. Then another, and another...

At last, he saw the water rise up near him, and after casting in a few more pebbles he was able to quench his thirst and save his life.

Little by little does the trick.

The Two Pots

There were once two pots that had been left on the bank of a river. One was made of brass and the other of earthenware. As the tide rose, they both floated off down the stream. They were tossed this way and that way by the current, and the earthenware pot tried its best to keep away from the brass one. Then the brass one cried out, "Don't worry my friend, I will not hit you."

8

"But I may bash into you by accident," said the earthenware pot. "Whether I hit you, or you hit me, you'll be fine, but I will suffer for it."

Equals make the best friends.

The Bundle of Sticks

There was once an old man who had several sons. When he knew that his time to die was near, he gathered all his sons together to give them some parting advice.

The man ordered his servants to bring in a bundle of sticks, and then he said to his eldest son, "See if you can break this." The son strained and strained, but with all his efforts was unable to break the bundle.

Then the old man asked another son to try... and another... and another... They all did their utmost, but none of them were successful.

"Now untie the sticks," said the father, and the sons did so. He instructed each of them to take a single stick. When they had done so, the dying man called out to them, "Now, try and break them." This time, the sons could all break what was in their hands with hardly any effort at all.

"Now you see my meaning," said their father, glad he had left his sons with a gift of wisdom.

Strength lies in united numbers.

11

The Boy
and the
Nettle

A **little boy was once stung** by a nettle. He ran
home crying to his mother and said, "It really
hurts me even though I only touched it gently."

"Ah, that is why," said the boy's mother,
soothingly. "If you touch a nettle again, grasp it
boldly, and it will be gentle to your hand, and
not hurt you in the least."

Whatever you do, do with all your might.

The Fox
and the
Mosquitoes

There was once a fox who tried to cross a river and was nearly swept away. He swam for his life and managed to grab a low-hanging branch with his jaws, to drag himself to shore. But as he hauled himself onto the bank, his tail became tangled in a bush, and he couldn't move.

A number of mosquitoes saw that the fox was trapped and came and settled on him. They began feasting on him, biting and sucking his blood, and the fox could do nothing at all to get away from their attack.

After a while, a hedgehog came strolling by.
He took pity on the fox, and approaching him
said, "You are in a very bad way, neighbor. Shall I
relieve you by driving off those mosquitoes who
are sucking your blood?"

"Thank you, Master Hedgehog," said the fox,
"but I would rather you didn't. Please leave them

all just where they are."

"Why, how is that?" asked the hedgehog.

"Well, you see," replied the fox, "these mosquitoes have been here a while and have had their fill. If you drive them away, others will come with fresh appetites and bleed me to death."

It's better to choose the lesser of two evils.

15

The Horse
and the
Mule

There was once a horse and a mule whose owners were traveling down a road. The horse belonged to a knight, and pranced along proudly. However, the mule belonged to a peasant. It plodded along, laden down with a bundle of firewood on its back. "I wish I were you," sighed the mule to the horse, "well fed

and groomed, and
with splendid harnessing."

At the end of the day, it was time
for the peasant and the knight to part
company. The mule enviously watched the horse
strut away.

Little did the mule know that the horse was
off to war. The next day, the horse had to carry
the knight into a great battle. The fighting was
ruthless, and the horse was in the thick of it. In
the final charge, the horse was badly wounded,
and left lying in agony among the dead.

Soon afterwards, the mule was led past. He

looked in horror at the remains of the battle and was shocked to see the horse on the point of death. "I was wrong," gasped the mule. "Better humble safety than this fancy danger."

Better to be lowly and safe than important and in danger.

The Farmer
and
Fortune

Once upon a time, a farmer was out ploughing his fields. All at once, his plough hit something solid, which would not budge. The farmer had to stop his horses and fetch a shovel to dig up whatever was in the way.

To his huge surprise, he dug up a pot of golden coins! Of course, he was overjoyed at his discovery. From then on, every day he went to pray at the shrine

of the Goddess of the Earth, to say thank you for his find. However, the Goddess of Fortune came to hear about this and was jealous.

She came to see the farmer and angrily demanded, "My man, why do you give Earth the credit for the gift that I gave to you? You have not once thought of thanking me for your good luck! However, should you be unlucky enough to lose what you have gained, I know very well that you would blame me, Fortune, for your bad luck."

Show gratitude where gratitude is due.

Jupiter
and the
Monkey

Long, long ago, when the world was new, the gods and goddesses of Mount Olympus ruled over everything. Once, the great god Jupiter who ruled over the Earth issued a proclamation to all the beasts. He offered a prize to the one who, in his judgment, produced the most beautiful offspring.

All the animals were so proud of their children that they were sure they would win the prize for themselves. They came in herds and flocks and swarms to make an enormous queue before

Jupiter to show him their babies.

Among them came the monkey, carrying her baby in her arms. It was a hairless, flat-nosed little thing, and when the gods saw it, they burst into laughter. However, the monkey hugged her baby and said, "Jupiter may give the prize to whoever he likes, but I shall always think my baby the most beautiful."

Beauty is in the eye of the beholder.

The Lion
and the
Hare

There was once a lion who was out hunting, prowling around the neighborhood looking for tasty morsels to eat. He was delighted when he came across a sleeping hare. He was just about to snap her up in his jaws when he saw a passing stag out of the corner of his eye. The lion at once left the hare and went after the bigger prize.

The lion chased and chased the stag for as long as he had strength, but he could not overtake him. In the end he had to abandon the attempt. "Never mind," he said to himself, "I shall go back and gobble up the hare after all."

The lion bounded back to where he had previously seen the hare. However, she was nowhere to be seen. He had to go home without dinner after all, with his tail between his legs.

"It serves me right," he said, "I should have been content with what I had, instead of hankering after a better prize."

Don't let greed cause you to overreach yourself, or you could lose all.

The Cage Bird and the Bat

There was once a tiny bird that lived in a cage, which hung outside a window. The little captive longed for the skies she could see through the bars, and even though she no longer had the joy of flying, she sang with the most beautiful voice. She would have gladdened the hearts of all who heard her — except that she sang at night, when everyone was asleep.

One night, a bat came and clung to the bars of the cage, and asked the bird why she was silent by day and sang only at night.

"I have a very good reason for only singing at night," said the bird. "It was once when I was singing in the daytime that a bird catcher was attracted by my voice, and he caught me. Since then I have only sung at night." But the bat replied, "It is no use doing that now, when you are a prisoner. If only you had done so before you were caught, you might still be free."

Precautions are useless after the event.

The Frogs
and the
Well

There were once two frogs who lived together in a marsh. It was damp and shady, with plenty of flies and worms to eat, just how they liked it. But one year the summer was very hot and dry. The marsh dried up, and the frogs were forced to leave and look for somewhere new to live.

They leapt and hopped for miles across the countryside, but all the ponds and lakes and streams and rivers were dried up like the marsh. The frogs had no option but to keep looking, for without water and shade they would dry up too.

Eventually they came to a deep well. One of them peered down into it — there was water at the bottom. The frog said to his friend, "This is the perfect place, let us jump in and settle here." But the other frog, who had a wiser head on his shoulders, replied, "Not so fast, my friend. Supposing this well dries up too, how should we get out again?"

Think twice before
you act.

The Town Mouse and the Country Mouse

Once upon a time, a town mouse went on a visit to his cousin in the country. He arrived at the country mouse's home to find that it was a barn, shared with other animals. The country mouse was delighted to see his relative, whom he loved very much, and made the town mouse heartily welcome. The country mouse was poor and lived a simple life. He was also quite rough and ready with his manners and habits. Beans and bacon, cheese and bread, and a bed of straw were all he had to offer the town mouse.

However the town mouse was used to living the high life in the city. He was accustomed to dining on much finer delicacies and sleeping in a much softer bed. He turned his nose up at this country fare and sleeping accommodation.

"I cannot understand," he said to his country cousin, "how you can put up with such poor food and sleeping on straw with farm creatures nearby. Come home with me and I'll show you how to live. When you have been in town a week you will wonder how you ever lived out here."

The country mouse was curious – after all, he had never seen the town and wondered what it would be like. So, the two mice set off together.

They arrived at the town mouse's residence late at night. It was a grand house, several stories high, with steps up to a big front door and down to a large cellar. As soon as the mice had squeezed into the cellar through a tiny hole in the bricks, the town mouse took his cousin into a splendid dining room. There, they found the remains of a fine feast on the table, and were soon eating jellies and cakes and all that was nice.

Suddenly the mice heard growling. "What is that?" asked the country mouse.

"It is only the dogs of the house," answered the town mouse in a calm voice.

"Only the dogs!" gasped the country mouse. "I do not like that kind of music at my dinner."

At that moment, the door flew open and in

came two huge dogs. The two terrified mice had to scamper down the table leg and run off.

"Goodbye, cousin," said the country mouse.

"What! Going so soon?" asked the town mouse in surprise.

"Yes," he replied. "Better beans and bacon in peace than cakes and ale in fear."

Better to live poorly in peace than richly in fear.

The Peacock
and
Hera

A **long, long time ago,** in the early days of the world, the gods and goddesses of Mount Olympus ruled over Earth, sky and sea. There was once a peacock who prayed earnestly to the goddess Hera, Queen of Mount Olympus. The peacock was more than happy with his beautiful looks,

35

which all the other birds envied, but he longed to have a better singing voice to go with it. He had quite an ugly cry, and what he really wanted was the voice of a nightingale.

However, the great Hera refused. The peacock would not take no for an answer and continued to beg. "Please grant me this," he pleaded, "after all, I am your favorite bird."

But Hera just replied, "Be content with what you have."

 One cannot be first in everything.

The Hares
and the
Frogs

There was once a time when the hares were disliked by all the other creatures. They made the hares' lives a misery by taunting and bullying them. The poor hares did not know what to do or where to go to escape from being tormented. Whenever the hares saw another animal approach them, off they would run.

One day a troop of wild horses came stampeding about by the hares, quite on purpose. In a total panic, the hares ran away, but the horses just followed, thundering about

with their crashing hooves.

The hares spent hours trying to escape, but to no avail – the horses would not give up. In the end, the despairing hares scuttled off to a nearby lake. They thought it was better to throw themselves in and drown rather than live in fear of being crushed to death by the horses.

But just as the hares approached the bank of the lake, a troop of frogs became frightened of them and scuttled off, jumping into the water.

This greatly surprised the hares, as they were so used to being frightened themselves.

"Truly," said one of the hares, "things are not as bad as they seem."

 There is always someone worse off than yourself.